Safe in a Storm

Text copyright © 2016 by Stephen R. Swinburne • Illustrations copyright © 2016 by Jennifer Bell • All rights reserved. Published by Scholastic Inc., *Publishers since 1920.* SCHOLASTIC, CARTWHEEL BOOKS, and associated logos are trademarks and/or registered trademarks of Scholastic Inc. • The publisher does not have any control over and does not assume any responsibility for author or third-party websites or their content. • No part of this publication may be reproduced, stored in a retrieval system, or transmitted in any form or by any means, electronic, mechanical, photocopying, recording, or otherwise, without written permission of the publisher. For information regarding permission, write to Scholastic Inc., Attention: Permissions Department, 557 Broadway, New York, NY 10012. • This book is a work of fiction. Names, characters, places, and incidents are either the product of the author's imagination or are used fictitiously, and any resemblance to actual persons, living or dead, business establishments, events, or locales is entirely coincidental. • Library of Congress Cataloging-in-Publication Data available • ISBN 978-0-545-86792-4 • 10 9 8 7 6 5 4 3 2 1   16 17 18 19 20 • Printed in Malaysia 108 • First edition, January 2016 • Book design by Esther Sarah Kim and Leslie Mechanic

Safe
in a
Storm

Written by **Stephen R. Swinburne**
Illustrated by **Jennifer A. Bell**

CARTWHEEL BOOKS
An Imprint of Scholastic Inc.

To teachers and school staff everywhere, who provide
a safe harbor for children every day . . . in memory
of the 20 Sandy Hook Elementary schoolchildren
-S.R.S.

To Vivi, Liam, and Elaina
-J.A.B.

When the storm rumbles loudly and the sky turns to ink,
Snuggle close, my little mole. Touch noses, warm and pink.

When the clouds grow darker and the rain pelts and stings,

I'm here, my little duck. Keep warm beside my wings.

As the storm begins to pound, making mountains of the sea,
Dive deep, my little whale. Swim safely next to me.

Across the savannah, clouds grow black and blue.

Don't worry, my little giraffe. I'll watch over you.

While the wind, rain, and mist hide the pack from view,

Close your eyes, my little wolf. I'm right here with you.

When the winds howl and blow with all their might,

Hang on, my little sloth. I've got you—hold tight.

While the raging storm bends every branch on the tree,
Snuggle close, my little owl, between the big tree and me.

The hurricane winds lash at the ledge where we hide.

Cuddle near, my little bobcat, safe by my side.

Across the meadow, the wild winds do not cease.

Nuzzle deep, my little lamb, close to my fleece.

The big gale sways our tree from side to side.
Be still, my little chimp. Pretend it's a ride.

The winds moan outside the den we have dug.

Hush now, my little bear. Inside, we're all snug.

The rain splashes around, making rivers run high.
Stay cozy, my little rabbit. Our burrow's all dry.

A storm will always end. Don't worry, and sleep tight.

I'll be right here, my little one. I love you. Good night!